Dear Parent:
Your child's love of reading starts here!

Every child learns to read in a different way and at his or her own speed. You can help your young reader improve and become more confident by encouraging his or her own interests and abilities. You can also guide your child's spiritual development by reading stories with biblical values and Bible stories, like I Can Read! books published by Zonderkidz. From books your child reads with you to the first books he or she reads alone, there are I Can Read! books for every stage of reading:

SHARED READING
Basic language, word repetition, and whimsical illustrations, ideal for sharing with your emergent reader.

BEGINNING READING
Short sentences, familiar words, and simple concepts for children eager to read on their own.

READING WITH HELP
Engaging stories, longer sentences, and language play for developing readers.

READING ALONE
Complex plots, challenging vocabulary, and high-interest topics for the independent reader.

ADVANCED READING
Short paragraphs, chapters, and exciting themes for the perfect bridge to chapter books.

I Can Read! books have introduced children to the joy of reading since 1957. Featuring award-winning authors and illustrators and a fabulous cast of beloved characters, I Can Read! books set the standard for beginning readers.

A lifetime of discovery begins with the magical words **"I Can Read!"**

Visit www.icanread.com for information on enriching your child's reading experience.
Visit www.zonderkidz.com for more Zonderkidz I Can Read! titles.

LORD, you have seen what is in my heart.
You know all about me.
—*Psalms 139:1*

The Best Breakfast
Copyright © 2008 by Mona Hodgson
Illustrations copyright © 2008 by Milena Jahier

Requests for information should be addressed to:
Zonderkidz, Grand Rapids, Michigan 49530

Library of Congress Cataloging-in-Publication Data

Hodgson, Mona Gansberg, 1954-
    The best breakfast / by Mona Hodgson ; illustrated by Milena Jahier.
        p. cm. -- (I can read ; level 2) (Desert critters series)
      ISBN 978-0-310-71740-9 (softcover)
      [1. Desert animals--Fiction. 2. Friendship--Fiction. 3. Christian life--Fiction.] I. Jahier,
      Milena, ill. II. Title.
    PZ7.H6649Bes 2008
    [E]--dc22

                                    2008008374

Art Direction & Design: Jody Langley

Printed in China

08 09 10 • 4 3 2 1

ZONDERkidz

I Can Read!

BEGINNING
1
READING

The Best Breakfast

story by Mona Hodgson

pictures by Milena Jahier

"Yippee!" Peck cheered.

The table was set.

The seed pancakes were ready.

Everything was just right.

Any minute now Peck's friends
would show up for breakfast.

When the doorbell rang,

Peck darted to the door.

Pokey stood on the top step.

"I brought cactus candy,"

said Pokey.

He held up a plate.

Peck didn't like cactus candy,
but he set it on the table anyway.

Hoppy showed up next.

She hopped in with a sack.

"I brought grass salad," she said.

Peck didn't like grass salad,

but he set it on the table anyway.

Then Speedy came.

He raced in with a pot.

He had brought food too.

Peck sighed.

"What did you bring?" he asked.

Speedy lifted the pot lid.

"I brought lizard soup," he said.

Peck didn't like lizard soup,

but he made room for it anyway.

Hunter wandered in last.

She didn't bring any food.

Peck was glad.

At least Hunter would enjoy

his seed pancakes.

Everyone sat down.

The friends started eating.

Peck looked over at Hunter.

Hunter wasn't eating pancakes.

Peck frowned.

Hunter was eating

the cactus flowers instead.

Peck crossed his wings.

He had wanted everything

to be just right.

Everything wasn't just right.

"You don't like my breakfast,"

Peck said.

"We don't always like
the same things," Hunter said.
"God said it's what's in our hearts
that matters," said Pokey.

"Peck, your kind heart
brought us all together,"
said Speedy.

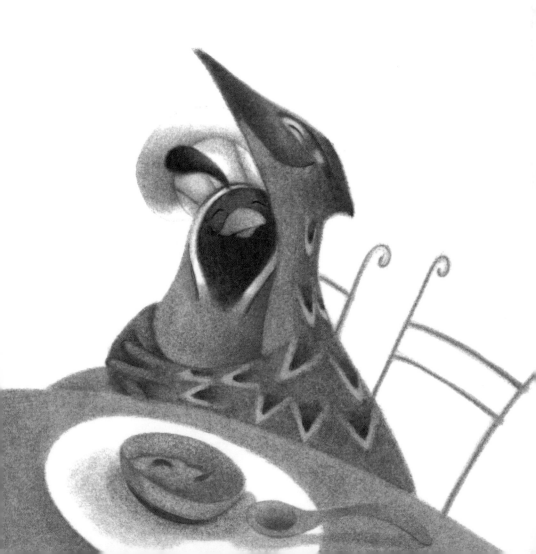

Hoppy ate grass salad.

"This is the best," she said.

Pokey chewed cactus candy.

"Yum. Yum," he said.

Speedy slurped lizard soup.

"Good soup," he said.

Hunter crunched cactus flowers.

"This is just right!" she said.

Peck took a bite of seed pancake.

He licked his beak.

"My breakfast is just right too,"
Peck said.

The friends all sat back

and patted their full tummies.

After breakfast,

the friends played games.

They laughed and had lots of fun.

"Yippee!" Peck cheered.

Breakfast was just right after all.